To my incredible husband, Terry, the best drummer I've ever known.
—V.K.

To all children affected by war.
Special thanks to
Patrick Schroeder, Gail Jarrow, Parker Lienhart, Candace Fleming,
Eric Rohmann, Miriam Busch and Andrew Day.
—L.D.

For Further Reading

Carter, Alice E., and Richard Jensen. The Civil War on the Web: A Guide to the Very Best Sites
(Completely Revised and Updated). Wilmington: SR Books, 2003.

Murphy, Jim. The Boys' War: Confederate and Union Soldiers Talk About the Civil War.
New York: Clarion Books, 1990.

Vaughan, Donald. The Everything Civil War Book: Everything You Need to Know About
the War That Divided the Nation. Avon, Mass.: Adams Media, 2000.

For a full bibliography, visit www.verlakay.com.

G. P. PUTNAM'S SONS · A division of Penguin Young Readers Group. Published by The Penguin Group.
Penguin Group (USA) Inc., 375 Hudson Street, New York, NY 10014, U.S.A.
Penguin Group (Canada), 90 Eglinton Avenue East, Suite 700, Toronto, Ontario M4P 2Y3, Canada (a division of Pearson Penguin Canada Inc.).
Penguin Books Ltd, 80 Strand, London WC2R 0RL, England.
Penguin Ireland, 25 St. Stephen's Green, Dublin 2, Ireland (a division of Penguin Books Ltd).
Penguin Group (Australia), 250 Camberwell Road, Camberwell, Victoria 3124, Australia (a division of Pearson Australia Group Pty Ltd).
Penguin Books India Pvt Ltd, 11 Community Centre, Panchsheel Park, New Delhi - 110 017, India.
Penguin Group (NZ), 67 Apollo Drive, Rosedale, Auckland 0632, New Zealand (a division of Pearson New Zealand Ltd).
Penguin Books (South Africa) (Pty) Ltd, 24 Sturdee Avenue, Rosebank, Johannesburg 2196, South Africa.
Penguin Books Ltd, Registered Offices: 80 Strand, London WC2R 0RL, England.

Design by Marikka Tamura. Text set Clarendon MT Std.
The paintings were done in watercolor and gouache over ink and pencil on 300lb cold press watercolor paper.
Library of Congress Cataloging-in-Publication Data
Kay, Verla. Civil War drummer boy / Verla Kay ; illustrated by Larry Day. p. cm.
Summary: When the Confederate Army calls, Johnny puts aside playing games with his sisters and leaves his plantation home to serve
as a drummer boy. 1. United States—History—Civil War, 1861–1865—Juvenile fiction. [1. Stories in rhyme.
2. United States—History—Civil War, 1861–1865—Fiction. 3. Drummers (Musicians)—Fiction.]
I. Day, Larry, 1956– ill. II. Title. PZ8.3.K225Civ 2012 [E]—dc23 2011020679
ISBN 978-0-399-23992-2
2 4 6 8 10 9 7 5 3 1

AUTHOR'S NOTE

In December of 1860, the Southern states began seceding from the United States of America, and on April 12, 1861, the first shots in the War Between the States were fired. It was the bloodiest war ever fought on American soil, and sometimes even brothers and cousins fought against one another on different sides of the war.

While researching this book, I was astonished to learn that some nights the soldiers from both sides, Blue (the Northern Union) and Gray (the Southern Confederate), would get together and play music in impromptu jam sessions. Then the next day they would resume fighting each other!

Boys as young as ten rushed to join the war, and one Union boy who was only nine enlisted with his father. Many soldiers were fourteen and fifteen and often the youngest became drummer boys, tapping out instructions for the troops as well as encouragement.

One of the most fascinating jobs of the drummer boys involved gas-filled observation balloons. A soldier would float above the landscape, spot the enemy, and use arm motions to let an officer on the ground know where they were. The officer would then have a drummer boy relay his orders to the troops. The Union Army built a fleet of balloons, but the Confederates had a much smaller budget, so they resourcefully made their hot-air balloons from brightly colored pieces of dress-length silk.

Confederate General Robert E. Lee officially surrendered on April 9, 1865, and the long and bloody war was finally over. The United States was still intact and slavery was soon abolished with the Thirteenth Amendment. Hooray for the United States of America! Long may it live as a country for free men.   —V.K.

Shady porches,
Fragrant breeze.
Clinging vines,
Magnolia trees.

Johnny running,
Kick-the-hoop.
Jumping, playing,
Hollers, "Whoop!"

Sisters squealing,
Jump aside.
Laughing, giggles,
Watch with pride.

Home, plantation,
Cotton, white.
Black slaves labor
Morn till night.

Business, culture,
Slavery.
North and South states
Disagree.

New election,
Government.
States elect a
President.

SOUTHERNERS
UNITE!

NORTHERN STATES
ELECT PRESIDENT

PROTECT YOUR HOME
AND FIRESIDE!!!

With his hopes high,
Lincoln leads.
Can't prevent it—
South secedes.

Fight for Dixie—
"Slaves must stay!"
Rebel soldiers
Wearing gray.

Army calling,
"We need YOU!"
Johnny joining,
Drumsticks, new.

Johnny, practice,
Tap, tap, tap.
Every signal
Has a rap.

Some for fighting,
One, "Wake up!"
One beat tells men,
"Time to sup."

Johnny drumming,
Breaking camp.
Rat, tat, tat, tat,
Soldiers tramp.

Smoking cannons,
Bayonets.
Lines of soldiers,
Marching steps.

Soldiers shooting,
Rifles aimed.
Bullets buzzing,
Bodies maimed.

Battle ceases,
End of day.
Nighttime jamming,
Blue and gray.

Johnny ponders,
Asks a friend,
"Will this long war
EVER end?"

Morning dawning,
Fight resumes.
Cannons, rifles,
Smoky plumes.

Hot air rising,
Silk cloth fills.
Basket floating,
Topping hills.

Union army
Down below.
"Where's their cannons?
We must know."

Cannons hidden
In the trees.
Soldier pinpoints
Enemies.

Waves his signals.
"Johnny, come!
Tap this message
On your drum!"

Johnny drumming,
Not too near.
Drumbeats echo,
Soldiers hear.

Cannons blasting,
Smoke-filled sky.
Fierce-fought battle,
Soldiers die.

Weary army
Must retreat.
Johnny, drumming,
Slows his beat.

LEE SURRENDERS!

"Lee Surrenders!"
Headline reads.
"War Has Ended!"
"South Concedes!"

Johnny tramping,
Crossing fields.
Manors looted,
Battlefields.

Passing slave huts,
Hurries fast.
"There it is,
Home at last!"

Johnny's family
Sells some lands.
Now their slaves are
Hired hands.

Rows of cotton,
Prickly, white.
Picked by workers,
Bundles tight.

Life is different,
War's to blame.
Only some things
Stay the same.

Shady porches,
Fragrant breeze.
Clinging vines,
Magnolia trees.